You Have Feelings
⇒ All the Time ⇐

Deborah Farmer Kris

Illustrated by Jennifer Zivoin

free spirit
PUBLISHING®

Library of Congress Cataloging-in-Publication Data
Names: Kris, Deborah Farmer, author. | Zivoin, Jennifer, illustrator.
Title: You have feelings all the time / Deborah Farmer Kris ; illustrated by Jennifer Zivoin.
Description: Minneapolis : Free Spirit Publishing Inc., 2022. | Series: All the time | Audience: Ages 2–6
Identifiers: LCCN 2021004435 (print) | LCCN 2021004436 (ebook) | ISBN 9781631985096 (hardcover) |
    ISBN 9781631985102 (pdf) | ISBN 9781631985119 (epub)
Subjects: LCSH: Emotions—Juvenile literature. | Emotions in children—Juvenile literature.
Classification: LCC BF723.E6 K75 2022 (print) | LCC BF723.E6 (ebook) | DDC 155.4/124—dc23
LC record available at https://lccn.loc.gov/2021004435
LC ebook record available at https://lccn.loc.gov/2021004436

Free Spirit Publishing does not have control over or assume responsibility for author or third-party websites and their content.

Reading Level Grade 1; Interest Level Ages 2–6;
Fountas & Pinnell Guided Reading Level I

Edited by Cassandra Sitzman
Cover and interior design by Emily Dyer

10 9 8 7 6 5 4 3 2 1
Printed in China
R18860921

Free Spirit Publishing Inc.
6325 Sandburg Road, Suite 100
Minneapolis, MN 55427-3674
(612) 338-2068
help4kids@freespirit.com
freespirit.com

FSC
www.fsc.org
MIX
Paper from
responsible sources
FSC® C144853

For Mike,
who makes room
for all my feelings

Happy, angry, sad, and scared,
excited and surprised.

You're full of feelings every day.
Your heart is super-sized!

You have feelings all the time.

Sometimes you sport a goofy grin,
and everything seems funny!

But sometimes you feel grumpy till
there's food inside your tummy.

You have feelings all the time.

You might feel a bit nervous
when you join a brand-new class.

You might also feel excited:
The first day's here at last!

You have feelings all the time.

You build the coolest, tallest tower!
Your chest fills up with pride.

Wibble, wobble, wobble, crash!
You want to run and hide.

You have feelings all the time.

When you put on a cape or wings,
you feel brave and strong.

And when you meet a brand-new friend,
you feel like you belong.

You have feelings all the time.

If classmates fight, you might feel scared, frustrated, or annoyed.

Then they start to laugh and play!
You twirl around with joy.

You have feelings all the time.

Sometimes, when a friend is blue,
your heart's unhappy too.

When they start to smile again,
you want to shout, "Woohoo!"

You have feelings all the time.

Feelings also come in twos:
you're happy AND you're sad.

You're glad that mom is
coming home, but when
grandma leaves,
you're mad.

You have feelings all the time.

At times you're like a peaceful bird
that's gliding through the air.

Or you might have a storm inside.
You want to stomp and glare!

You have feelings all the time.

Sharing what you feel inside
can help you settle down.

A warm hug or a gentle smile
can turn a frown around.

You have feelings all the time.

Stories can be scary, silly,
surprising, or delightful.

When you cozy up to read,
nothing seems too frightful.

You have feelings all the time.

Neighbors, teachers, parents, friends
have lots of feelings too.

We laugh and cry; we smile and sigh.
We *feel* . . . just like you!

We ALL have feelings all the time.

⇉ A Letter to Caregivers ⇇

When my daughter was two, she was terrified of houseflies. Every time a fly buzzed near her, she would scream. After a few rough days, I had an idea. What if we named the fly "Bob"? What if we gave Bob a personality—a favorite color, a favorite food, a reason for visiting our house.

It worked. Instead of screaming, she began saying, "Hi, Bob. You came back!"

So much of my parenting and teaching comes down to some version of Bob the Fly: First, you name it. Name the feeling you are experiencing—whether it's fear, sadness, anger, or excitement. If we can name it, we can talk about it.

I often draw inspiration from Fred Rogers, who spoke to children clearly, calmly, and concretely about emotions. "Anything that's human is mentionable, and anything that is mentionable can be more manageable," he once wrote. "When we can talk about our feelings, they become less overwhelming, less upsetting, and less scary." Helping young children develop an emotional vocabulary is powerful. In this book, you've found depictions of over a dozen emotions. You've seen children feeling happy, angry, sad, scared, excited, surprised, silly, grumpy, proud, frustrated, confident, connected, worried, relieved, peaceful, comforted, and loved.

Young children have big feelings *all the time*. When we help them recognize and name those feelings, we help them learn to manage their feelings in the moment—an important life skill. Here are a few ideas you can try in your home or classroom.

Four Ideas for Helping Children Manage Big Feelings

1. Name Emotions

Toddlers and preschoolers have limited (but growing!) expressive language skills. Caregivers can "listen" to children's behavior—be it yelling, pushing, crying, or withdrawing—and help them put a name to what they are feeling. Sometimes we want to jump to a solution, but it's important to first acknowledge the emotion. This might sound like:

- "You look mad. Your friend scribbled on your picture, and that doesn't feel good."

- "You look sad. You forgot to bring your stuffy for naptime, and I know how much you love that stuffy. It's okay to feel sad."

As children mature, you can use this strategy to introduce more nuanced feelings to build their emotional vocabulary: "You sound frustrated. Your tower fell down and you worked hard to make it tall! That's disappointing." Or, "You look startled. That thunder was really loud, and it surprised you."

Sometimes you will get it wrong! And as children get better at understanding and expressing emotions, that can be a great conversation starter. As my eight-year-old daughter told me the other day, "I'm not mad, Mom, I'm nervous. Sometimes when I'm nervous, I act mad." Me too!

2. Normalize Emotions

It's important not to classify emotions as good or bad. We all have feelings all the time, and they are all normal. Even so, strong emotions can scare or overwhelm children, so normalizing their reactions—helping them see that everyone feels mad, sad, or scared sometimes—can comfort them and build their perspective-taking skills.

Try this: after the child has calmed down, circle back and briefly summarize what happened, including how the child felt. Then, remind the child that everyone—including you—feels this way sometimes.

This might sound like:

> "When grandma left this morning, it seemed like you felt very sad and mad. You kicked me and cried. You wanted grandma to stay and play with you. Everyone feels sad and mad sometimes. I felt sad when grandma left too. I like talking with her and watching her read books to you. Do you want to draw her a picture or call her tomorrow to say hello?"

As you revisit emotional events, don't be surprised if a child wants to hear the story about "the time I got mad at the grocery store" multiple times. But such repetition has its benefits. With the triggering event safely in the past, you and the child can use it as a reference point to talk about how they are growing in their ability to manage their emotions.

3. Practice Emotional Regulation Skills

We can't always control how we feel, but we can make choices about what we *do* when we have strong feelings. That's called emotional regulation. When children are feeling intense emotions—such as anger, frustration, or fear—they tend to have less impulse control. But once those emotions start to settle, it's easier to problem-solve with them and to practice self-regulation skills. Here are a few strategies to help calm these emotional storms.

My favorite technique for both children and adults is mindful breathing. When we are upset, our breathing often becomes fast and shallow. It's a normal biological response to stress. But when we take deep breaths through our nose, we send a message back to the brain: "It's okay to calm down." In moments of peace, practice these breathing strategies with children, and then guide them to use the strategies when big feelings arise:

- Birthday Cake: Pretend your fingers are birthday candles and blow them out one by one.

- Breathing Buddies: Lie on your back, put a favorite stuffed animal on your tummy, and watch that animal slowly move up and down as you inhale and exhale.

- Square Breathing: Breathe in through the nose to the count of four. Hold the breath to the count of four. Breathe out to the count of four. Then hold to the count of four. Repeat two or three times. Counting can help children focus their mind on breathing and distract them from stressors.

Here are two more activities that build children's emotional regulation toolboxes:

- The ability to press pause and stay grounded during emotional peaks is a great self-regulation skill. To practice this, take a "senses walk" around a local park or neighborhood. What do children see, smell, feel, and hear? Practice pausing for a short time and quietly focusing on one sense: "Let's stop and just listen for one minute. What do you hear?" Then share observations.

- Every day has its highs and lows—its pleasant and less pleasant emotions. To help children understand this, take turns at mealtime or bedtime sharing the ups and downs of the day in a concrete way. For example, share one moment when you felt happy or excited and one moment when you felt upset. This reminds children that even adults have feelings all the time, and it gives you an opportunity to share with children how you respond to sadness, worry, and frustration.

4. "Read" Pictures

Reading is a great tool for learning about emotions, and picture books offer an additional tool for teaching emotional literacy: illustrations. When a happy, scary, or frustrating event occurs in a story, pause and look at the picture together. Say, for example, "Look at them—how do you think they are feeling right now?" Examine characters' facial expressions, their body language, and what they are doing. You can use this same technique when you watch movies, shows, or videos together.

These strategies work best when we, as adults, model them. Children take their emotional cues from us, so talk about how you are feeling and why. Share what you do to feel better and calm down when you are sad, mad, or scared. Practice mindfulness with children. And curl up and read a good book together—an activity that is sure to help children feel safe and loved!

—**Deborah Farmer Kris**

About the Author and Illustrator

Deborah Farmer Kris is a child development expert and parent educator. She serves as a columnist and consultant for PBS KIDS and writes for NPR's *MindShift* and other national publications. Over the course of her career, Deborah has taught almost every grade K–12, served as a school administrator, directed leadership institutes, and presented to hundreds of parents and educators around the United States. Deborah and her husband live in Massachusetts with their two kids—who love to test every theory she's ever had about child development. Mostly, she loves sharing nuggets of practical wisdom that can help kids and families thrive.

Jennifer Zivoin has illustrated more than forty children's books, and her art has appeared in children's magazines, including *High Five* and *Clubhouse Jr.* She illustrated the *New York Times* and #1 *Indiebound* best seller *Something Happened in Our Town.* The Children's Museum of Indianapolis, the world's largest children's museum, featured her art in a special *Pirates and Princesses* exhibit. Jennifer provided artwork for celebrity picture books, including those by James Patterson and Guns N' Roses. Recently, Jennifer made her debut as an author with her book *Pooka & Bunni.* Jennifer lives in Indiana with her husband, daughters, and pet chinchillas.

Other Great Books from Free Spirit

I'm Happy-Sad Today
Making Sense of Mixed-Together Feelings
by Lory Britain, Ph.D., illustrated by Matthew Rivera
For ages 3–8. 40 pp.; HC; full-color; 11¼" x 9¼".

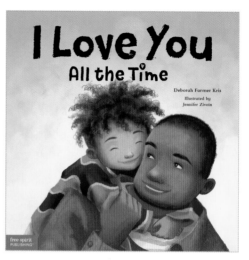

I Love You All the Time
by Deborah Farmer Kris, illustrated by Jennifer Zivoin
For ages 2–6. 32 pp.; HC; full-color; 10" x 10".

F Is for Feelings
by Goldie Millar and Lisa A. Berger, illustrated by Hazel Mitchell
For ages 3–8. 40 pp.; PB and HC; full-color; 11¼" x 9¼".

I Feel
A book about recognizing and understanding emotions
by Cheri J. Meiners, M.Ed., illustrated by Penny Weber
For ages 2–4. 24 pp.; BB; full-color; 7" x 7";
includes digital content.